MW01069445

PRINCESS PINECONE
AND THE
WEE ROYALS

By C.C. Bernstein
Stitchings by Irem Yazici

Princess Pinecone was the size of a grain of rice. Her home was a tiny pinecone, which is why her name was Princess Pinecone, and she had four friends:

Wherever you go, there you are.

For my loving and wise mother who
introduced me to Princess Pinecone
long ago.

Princess Pinecone
and the
Wee Royals

Duchess Daffodil,

Archduke Acorn,

Lady Log,

and Lord Lilypad.

When the early birds sang, the wee royals would eat daisy pancakes together and watch the sun rise.

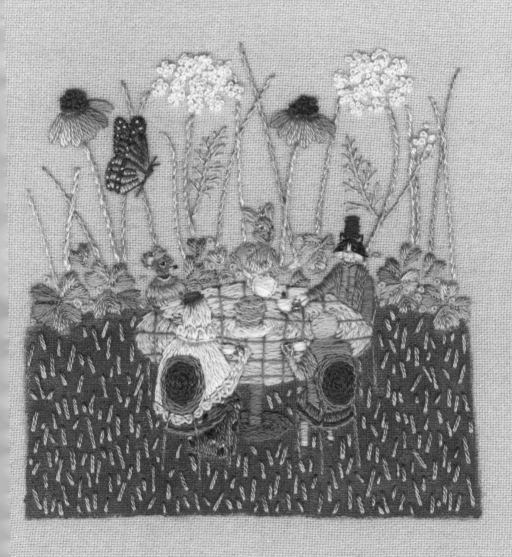

One morning, they found a grey ball
beside their daisy basket.

The Archduke kicked it and the ball
yelped for it was a wee man! A wee man
with a curly grey beard and curly shoes.

"Did you eat all our daisies?" asked Lady Log hands on her hips.

"I did," said the wee man. "I'm sorry. I didn't know they were yours and I was so hungry."

"Well now we're hungry," said the Duchess.

"I'm starving," moaned the Archduke.

"I say, let's lock this thief up!" said the Lord.

"Calm down everyone," said the Princess. "Wee man, what is your name?"

"Yairf Dogratherf," he said.

"An interesting name," said the Princess.

"A ridiculous name," said the Lady.
"The name of a thief," said the Lord.
"I'm FAMISHED!" said the Duchess.
"Fine," said the Princess. "If you're
going to be mean, we'll have our breakfast someplace else. Now Yairf, where
did you say you're from?"

Yairf was a great storyteller and a good fisherman. He and the Princess laughed and laughed.

They ate fried plankton for breakfast
and sipped on honeysuckle tea.

The Princess woke up with two lumps
on her shoulders the next day. They
didn't hurt so she ignored them.

When she brought plankton to the others and tried to make peace, they shook their heads and called her a hunchback.

The next morning the rest of the wee
royals woke up with lumps on their
shoulders too but their lumps hurt like
stubbed toes.
"My humps my humps my huuuuumps!"
cried the Lord.

The Duchess was the only one who didn't whine. She searched for medicinal plants like four leaf clovers to help them feel better.

When the Princess offered to help, the Duchess felt a different type of pain. They had been so awful to the Princess and here she was, smiling, lending a hand.

"I'm so sorry," said the Duchess and she meant it.

They found Yairf polishing his shoes.

"I'm really sorry Yairf," said the Duchess, "Do you think we could ever be friends?"

"Yes my dear," said Yairf. "Don't cry.
Find me two four leaf clovers and all is
forgiven."

"I wish I could," said the Duchess.
"We just searched and found none."

"Sometimes," he said, pointing to two nearby clovers. "the things you need are hiding right under your nose.

The Duchess picked the clovers and laid them at Yairf's feet and that's when her lumps began to move. The Princess's did too.

They ran to the others. Everyone
twisted and turned as their lumps
wobbled like puddings and then...
and then...

The lumps hatched wings! The Lady,
the Archduke and the Lord's wings
were small and cobwebby. They only
lifted a few inches off the ground.

But the Princess and the Duchess
floated up and up on wings full of
hope.

They soared high above the treetops
where Yairf was waiting for them.
There was no pain anymore, only joy.

"Yairf are we fairies?" asked the
Duchess.

"We are my dear. I'm your Fairy
Godfather, to be exact."

Fairy Godfather... Yatrf Dogratherf...
Fairy Godfather, thought the Princess,
has the same letters...

"Your name has the same letters as Fairy Godfather!" she exclaimed.

"TA DA!" said Yairf. Then quietly. "I love that part."

There were endless hills in the distance.
They had always thought their glade
was the only one.

The Princess and the Duchess had so many questions but before they could ask even one Yairf squeezed their hands "Have courage and be kind," he said, before disappearing like a dewdrop in the sun.

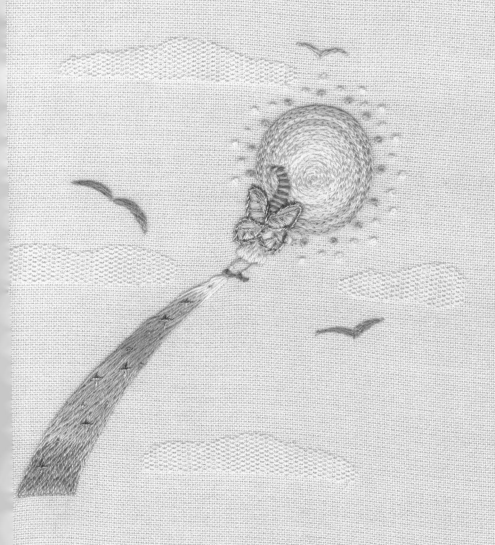

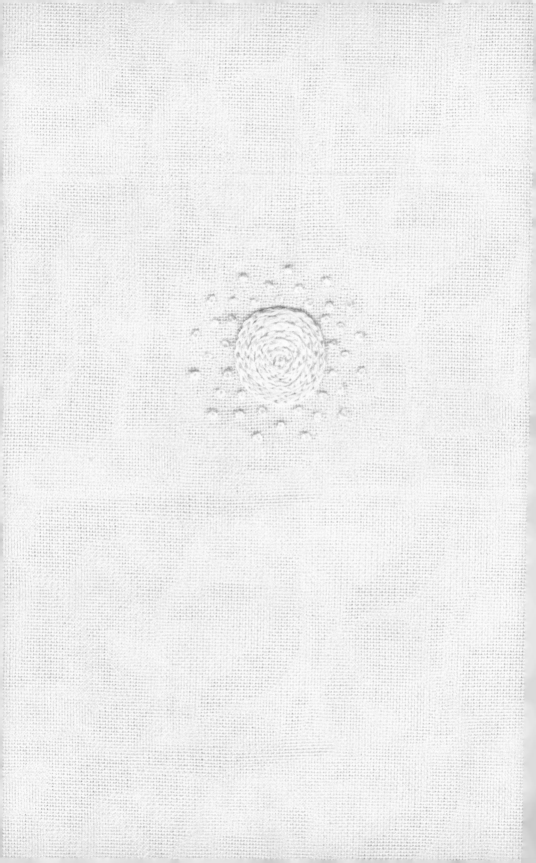

The end, but really, the beginning.

TETON MOUNTAIN PUBLISHING

First published by Teton Mountain Publishing in 2020

Teton Mountain Publishing
P.O. Box 242
Teton Village, WY 83025

WWW.TETONMOUNTAINPUBLISHING.COM

ISBN 978-1-7357328-1-7

CPSIA information can be obtained
at www.ICGtesting.com
Printed in the USA
BVHW021047250121
598674BV00017B/168